P9-CQF-526

Brian Pinkney

Time for Kenny

GREENWILLOW BOOKS
An Imprint of HarperCollinsPublishers

For information address HarperCollins Children's Books,
a division of HarperCollins Publishers,
195 Broadway, New York, NY 10007.
www.harpercollinschildrens.com

The images were painted with Golden fluid acrylic and
india ink on 300 Series Strathmore watercolor paper.
The text type is 26-point Avenir 55 Roman.

Library of Congress Cataloging-in-Publication Data

Names: Pinkney, J. Brian, author, illustrator.
Title: Time for Kenny / Brian Pinkney.
Description: First edition. | New York, NY :
Greenwillow Books, an imprint of HarperCollinsPublishers, [2021] |
Audience: Ages 4 up. | Audience: Grades K-1. |
Summary: During his busy day, Kenny gets dressed,
fights his fear of the vacuum cleaner, gets a soccer lesson from his sister,
and prepares for bed, with his loving family always near.
Identifiers: LCCN 2020035105 | ISBN 9780060735289 (hardcover)
Subjects: CYAC: Day—Fiction. | Family life—Fiction. | African Americans—Fiction.
Classification: LCC PZ7.P63347 Tim 2021 | DDC [E]—dc23
LC record available at https://lccn.loc.gov/2020035105

First Edition

20 21 22 23 24 25 RTLO 10 9 8 7 6 5 4 3 2 1

Greenwillow Books

For Dobbin

It is time for Kenny to get dressed for the day.

Can he wear this shirt?
No, that's Daddy's shirt.

Can he wear these shoes?
No, those are Mommy's shoes.

Can he wear these shorts?
No, silly, those are his sister's shorts.

Can he wear this hat?
No, that is Grandaddy's hat.

Time to take Grandaddy to the bus.
Is Kenny dressed?

Yes!

Kenny doesn't like the vacuum cleaner.
It sleeps in the closet.

It roars like a lion.

It eats Kenny's chips.

It eats Kenny's cereal.

Could it eat Kitty?

Could it eat Kenny?

No. It can't eat Kenny.

But Daddy might tickle him!

Kenny's sister is teaching him soccer. "No hands!" she says.

Kenny tries to kick the ball with his right foot.

He tries to kick it with his left foot.

He falls on it.

He rides it.

He tries to pick it up.
"No hands!"

Kenny uses his knee.

He uses his head.

He kicks the ball high.

He kicks the ball low.

He kicks it right.

He kicks it left.

And sometimes

he makes a goal!

Kenny's bedtime is in five minutes.
But Kenny is not tired.

It is four minutes before Kenny goes to bed.
But Kenny is not tired.

Three minutes until Kenny goes to bed.
But Kenny is not tired.

Two minutes before Kenny has to go to bed.
But Kenny is not tired.

One minute until bedtime!
But Kenny still isn't tired.

Time for bed.

"I'm tired," says Kenny.

"But you can read me a book!"